We are lions,
and we like to prowl.

We are wolves,
and we like to howl.

We are pigeons,
and we like to coo.

We are cows,
and we like to . . .

... *dig.*

. . . blow enormous bubbles.

But we love blowing enormous bubbles! Look! We're attempting a new world record!

We are frogs,
and we like to swim.

We are shrimp,
and we like to ski.

Hmmm. Well, what do *you* think, ladies and
gentlemen, boys and girls?
It will probably sound very silly.
And it won't rhyme, you know.
Are you sure you want to hear what the
animals really like?
Oh! OK then. From the top. A-one, a-two,
a-one, two, three, and . . .

We are lions, and we like . . . flower arranging.

We are wolves,
and we like to perform magic!

We are pigeons,
and we like ballet.

We are cows,
and we like to dig.

We are monkeys,
and we like all-you-can-eat buffets.

We are frogs, and we like tennis and most martial arts. Our favorite food is pizza with extra mushrooms, but with absolutely no tomatoes whatsoever.

We are shrimp, and we like to ski.

Not acrobatics?

Cheese?
You actually
like cheese?

Or cheerleading?

Or Modern Art?

No, we really do like cheese!

Right,
that's it!
Show's
over!

No!
Please
let us
finish!

But I don't like flowers.

PERFORMANCE TONIGHT ONLY

WHAT ANIMALS REALLY LIKE

Composed & Conducted by TIMBERTEETH

Lyrics & Pictures by FIONA ROBINSON

* * * * * * ABRAMS BOOKS FOR YOUNG READERS, LONDON *

For Mum & Dad. – F.R.

Ladies and gentlemen! Boys and girls!
Here, for the first time, I present my new song,

Ladies and gentlemen! Boys and girls!
Here, for the first time, I present my new song,